The Princess of the Enchanted Forest

Philip Antony

Book Cover by Mackenzie Rose Ridgeway

For my beloved Sara Jean –

My editor, best friend, and soul mate

Acknowledgments

I wish to thank the many people who contributed to bringing this story to fruition. Thanks to Jimmy Cieslewicz for taking the time to read the manuscript early on, and for the numerous recommendations to help launch this story. A special note of acknowledgement and appreciation to Charlize Tulimieri for her invaluable suggestions, for the important edits, and especially for the input that only a young adult can provide. This story would not have come to fruition were it not for Charlize.

Also, a huge thank you to the illustrator, Mackenzie Rose Ridgeway for the cover art.

It is with enormous gratitude mixed with sadness that I acknowledge the invaluable contribution of Sara Jean who was my first and most critical editor; who helped with the numerous re-writes; and who gave me the encouragement to continue to write not only this story, but many others. Sadly, she is no longer with me, and will be sadly missed as my best editor, best friend and life partner.

Table of Contents

PROLOGUE

As the sun rose over the distant horizon, the night sky changed from deep blue to a warm orange. Wisps of high clouds traced lazy patterns as they reflected the morning glow. It was the beginning of yet another suffocating, hot day in the rainforest. The jungle below resembled a dense green, rolling carpet, so dense that the morning light could not penetrate the darkness beneath its canopy. And that gave the night hunters a little more time to complete their gruesome task: stalking and hunting their prey, before retreating into their cool dens to feast on the night's conquest.

As the sun rose higher in the sky, the forest floor surrendered the cool air that now rose to condense into a thick milky mist that covered the treetops. It rolled down the hills and hovered over the great Amazon River. In the dim light of the forest below this misty blanket, the daily struggle of the creatures of the forest to survive had begun. Theirs was a continuous, desperate struggle to live out their lives staying one step ahead of the predators. The rising steam from the heat of the morning only muted the growls, groans, hisses and screams of the hunter-killers, who in turn were killed, only to be exterminated by a higher order of predator. It was an unbroken cycle without sympathy or pity.

But this rainforest was different; it was no ordinary place. Some said it was enchanted; some said it was haunted and punished by the spirits. The Arawakan tribal elders spoke of a little girl who was abandoned at a river's edge. Her parents left the little child to die in the jungle because the village witch doctor declared that she was possessed by an evil spirit – the Shadow God. The jungle had been besieged for many days and nights with violent storms, floods, fires and attacks from the jungle predators. Many of the villagers disappeared – taken by the violent storms or fled in terror.

Despite the curse of the witch doctor, some days later, the villagers regretted their harsh decision and set out to find the beautiful little girl. They searched for days and weeks for her; they sought the help of other local villages with no success. The warriors could not find any evidence that she had been taken by predators.

She had disappeared without a trace.

The village elders said that her spirit wandered the rainforest for many years in search of her mother and father. Some said she was a ghost seeking revenge; some said she was turned into a fairy who made the forest her home. But there were others who said that these stories were the ramblings of old men – old goats that wanted to perpetuate the ancient legends and the old ways. The mystery of the little girl continued for many years. As the story was repeated from one generation to the next, it was said that there really was a girl, but she was no ordinary girl. She lived in the furthest depths of the rainforest. No one knew how she got there, and very few people had ever seen her. There were stories that she could speak to the birds and all the animals in the forest.

Some said she was young, and there were some who said she was old. Some said she was beautiful beyond words, wearing flowing silk that shone like the sun. Others described seeing a haggard woman wearing rags, draped in a faded blue blanket and stooped with age walking with a twisted cane.

The mystery of the haunted spirit or fairy, a young woman or old hag, was passed down from generation to generation. Mothers told their daughters who, in turn, told their daughters. Each described seeing one or the other of these visions.

Despite all attempts to find evidence or an explanation for this story, it remained a mystery… until now.

Chapter 1

It Begins Here

It all began here, in the most remote part of the Amazon rainforest.

Tucked in behind a stand of tall palm trees, there was a small, old village. The villagers were happy to be isolated from the strangers who came from the east in their smoking and noisy machines, desecrating their forest homeland. These outsiders did not respect the trees, the birds and the other sacred animals. Their only purpose was to cut the trees to make way for roads, cow pastures and fields of soybeans as far as the eye could see. Others came with dynamite to blow away the rocky places to be followed by giant shovels that scooped up the soil. These people searched for the same precious stones that the members of the tribe adorned themselves with or traded with other villages.

The villagers farmed their land for vegetables; they fished and hunted for meat. Their main crop was manioc or casava from which they made bread, cereal and pudding. Plantain, which resembles a banana – green and not as ripe, was another crop that grew there and a good source of nutrition. In addition, of course, the jungle itself provided them with an abundance of other fruits and vegetables. The nearby river was teeming with fish. The young warriors' first role was to provide fish and meat for the villagers. The river and the dense jungle could provide them with all they needed: tapir, deer, wild pig, agouti, alligator, sloth, monkey, and fish.

Hunting was not a sport; they hunted only to provide food for the village. It was often long and dangerous; a poisonous snake or an attacking wild pig could kill or maim a hunter. There was no joy in the kill. For the hunters, a successful hunt meant food for all the villagers. All the food, farmed or hunted, was shared equally among the people. In times of crisis when the crops failed, or when the animals had moved to higher ground during the rainy season, the people of one village would share with the other nearby villagers.

It was a peaceful and happy place. Chickens roamed free and so did the young children. For these infants, any adult was a father or mother. The older boys tended the cattle and pigs and learned the art of hunting and fishing. Young girls learned to cook, sew and practice medicine. More importantly, the women were also the keepers of the village business with other villages. They were also the source of the history and the traditions of the village. The warriors were the arms and legs; the women were the hearts and minds.

One early morning, the villagers awoke to a sinister and dreaded sign. There was no sun in the sky. It was hidden by dark, ominous clouds that cast a shroud over the entire forest. It was a bad omen; it was the year of the Shadow God. Day after day, month after month, darkness prevailed. Day became night; the only light was from cooking fires. Crops failed; farm animals died, and the streams turned to dust, taking the fish with it. Even the dense jungle could not provide plants and herbs. The jungle animals had disappeared. So great was the fear and despair of the villagers that many just wandered into the jungle and were never seen again. It was said that they were swallowed up by the Shadow God.

Despite their misery, today was a special day for the people of the village of Achaka. The cacique (chief) – Choco – called the villagers together to make an important announcement.

"My friends, though we have suffered much over the past days, we have good news! Today, our beloved friend, Sira, wife of Tulo, has given birth to a girl. Her name is to be Luci."

He walked over to Sira and picked up the newborn baby, who was wrapped in a beautiful blue blanket. Choco said, "My friends, I know how difficult it has been for us, but we must celebrate this new life even in the face of the darkness and death that surrounds us."

The chief removed the blue cloth that wrapped the baby and held her up for everyone to see. There were loud gasps followed by a stunned silence.

Luci was beautiful – beautiful beyond words. Her skin was smooth and delicate, pale pink in color and when it caught the light, it glowed like a blossom in the afternoon sun – an 'anacaona' in the Arawakan language. Her hair seemed spun with gold, her eyes, blue as the sky. Her cooing sounded like a baby 'Kodibio' (bird). The villagers had never seen such a baby. All the children in the village had lustrous brown skin, straight black silky hair, and large dark eyes instead.

One of the villagers called out, "It is a bad sign. The Shadow God continues to punish us. He has brought a monster in our midst."

Another frightened villager screamed, "She is an evil spirit, a daughter of the Shadow God, sister to the 'Ori' (snake)!"

"Kill it, Choco! She will only bring more misery to us."

"Put her in the bush. Send her back to the Shadow God," said another.

One after another, the villagers began to demand that the newborn child be left in the jungle to be taken by the creatures of the night. Choco was a good chief, a gentle man with children of his own. He could not believe that this was the work of the Shadow God. Surely, this was just a helpless child who had been born different. As a hunter, he had many times wandered to the edges of the deep jungle and had seen people of the same light skin color with different clothes, speaking different languages. But, at the same time, he was the tribal chief – the leader. The people looked to him as the caretaker of the traditions that stretched back into the recesses of time – the time of the First People. His primary responsibility was to keep the community together despite their suspicions and beliefs about this newborn baby. It must be kept together at all costs, even at the expense of sacrificing this helpless child. *What if word of this child reached the other villages?* he thought. He could only imagine the harsh reaction; it would fracture the fragile peace and tranquility of the jungle people who were already worn thin from this perilous year.

"I will think on it," he told the villagers.

The villagers were relentless in their demand that Luci be surrendered to the jungle and the Shadow God. In addition to the hardship they had suffered, now this — an evil being living in their midst. There was more fear that the Shadow God would visit them again to bring more terror. It was too much for them to bear. Not long after baby Luci was introduced to the village, the villagers began to shun Tulo and Sira. Day after day, they refused to share food and water with the couple. Tulo and his sons were forced to resort to hunting and fetching water for their family. Despite her just having a baby, the other women in the village would not help Sira with her duties as wife and mother, as was the custom to care for newborn children and their mothers. The people avoided Tulo's shelter; the women refused to allow Sira to join their daily meetings. Even their two sons were excluded from warrior training. Their judgment was that

Luci's parents either submit their child to the Shadow God or leave the village with the cursed child.

Chapter 2

When Ignorance and Fear Prevail

Luci's parents, Tulo and Sira, were terrified by the demands of the tribe, and at the same time, confused about the birth of such a beautiful but different child. Sira spoke first to her husband, "Tulo, she is our daughter. Yes, she is different, but I cannot believe that this innocent baby is a daughter of the Shadow God only because she was born with light skin. What can we do? I fear that we too will be banished into the jungle."

Tulo was a hard man – a fearless warrior who spent his days with the other warriors hunting for food, and occasionally fighting with other tribes. He was raised to be a warrior and was said to be the best hunter with a bow and blowgun. He was most likely to be the next chief and was both feared and admired by the other warriors. He was also steeped in the culture of his people.

He was a good husband, provider and father to his two sons. Now, he was a father to a little girl, a strange child with light skin and hair like corn silt. Unlike his two sons, little Luci was quiet and content to be near her mother. Her cooing was like a bird singing.

"My dear wife, I am proud to be the father of this child regardless of her skin and hair color, but we are also members of this village. As such, we must uphold the traditions and rules of our community. It grieves me, but I fear that we have no choice. We must also think of our sons. What will become of them? And you? The village women already avoid you. They will never allow you to look after their children. And that is nothing compared to what will happen to Luci. Is it not better that she be given up to the spirits of the jungle than to live our lives surrounded by fear, suspicion, and segregated from our community?"

He reached out to his wife; she was heartbroken. She knew and understood the traditions, including the fearsome Shadow God, but could not understand why this innocent child should be the victim of others' fears. She was just a baby after all.

"Is there nothing we can do, my husband? Why don't we leave this village and find another where we can live in peace, away from these cruel and hateful people? Surely, that is the least we can do for Luci. You are the bravest warrior and hunter. Any village would welcome you, and us."

Tulo hid the pain he felt, but instead tried to comfort Sira. "My beloved wife, do you really think that there is a village with open minds who would accept us with this child who is so different? And what of Luci? Do you think that the other children would be allowed to play with her, to sit with her to learn the arts, to share their food with her? No, my beloved, I fear that she would be shunned and beaten with sticks out of fear. Luci would only have us. Who would protect her when we are transported to the spirit world? Even our sons are wary of her and would surely abandon her when they marry."

Sira began to sob, "Please, husband, please, there must be another way. She is my child, *our* child. I cannot part with her. Please don't abandon her to the Shadow God."

Tulo loved Sira so much that he took her every wish to his heart, but this was a request that was beyond him to give. My beloved wife, "Let us seek the advice of our chief, Choco."

It was with a heavy heart that Choco rendered his judgment. "My beloved children, you know how much I love both of you. Tulo, you also know that when my time comes to leave this world, it is you who will succeed me, and become the chief of our people. You will carry the burden, the joy and responsibility not only of your family, but also of our larger family, the entire village, their families, and their future."

Choco continued, "If you were in my position, what would your judgment be – your family or the larger family, our people?"

Tulo bowed his head, acknowledging Choco's remark.

The chief then turned to Sira, "I love you like a daughter. My dear Sira, I know that you are suffering. I am supposed to possess the wisdom to make decisions that are for the good of all our people, but in this instance, I cannot. I have neither the wisdom nor the heart to decide for you. Both of you will be the next leaders of our people, and the guardians of the traditions and of the future. I must leave it to both of you to decide."

With that, he went over to Sira, put his arms around her, and kissed her gently on her cheek as his tears mixed with hers. He then put his hand on Tulo's shoulder and looked deeply into his eyes for a moment. Then, he turned and left.

Tulo knew what had to be done. He turned to Sira who was sobbing. She knew it as well. Trembling with grief and fear, she collapsed.

Chapter 3

The Fateful Decision

Several months later, Choco's wife came to Tulo and Sira in their shelter. She stood in front of the open hut with tears streaming down her face. "Choco is dead. My husband, our chief, is gone from us. Before his death, he told us that you are to lead our people. The villagers know what has happened; they must now look to you for comfort and guidance." She gestured for Tulo to come out from the hut. "Please, Tulo." As he did, Choco's wife knelt before Tulo, and kissed his hand, and said, "My chief."

As was the custom, the widow followed behind the new chief to the center of the village. "Our beloved cacique, my husband, Choco, has gone over to the spirit world, and has commanded that Tulo become our new cacique," she said.

The shaman, who was the spiritual elder of the village, came forward, and knelt before Tulo as a sign of his loyalty to the new chief. In his hand was a ring of blossoms. He then rose and put the crown of flowers on Tulo's head. He turned to the villagers and said, "Choco has gone to defend us against the Shadow God; Tulo will now lead us." Turning to the large crowd of villagers that had gathered in the center, the shaman raised both his arms and with a loud voice said, "Declare your allegiance to our new chief, Tulo."

"Not before he sends his evil white child back to the Shadow God. Only then will I pledge my allegiance," said one of the villagers.

Then another spoke up, "Tulo, my family will follow, but you must dispose of the cursed child. Only then can you be my chief."

With that, the chorus of demands to rid the village of little Luci grew louder and louder. Just as Choco had predicted, Tulo was faced with the most critical decision of his life – spare Luci and leave the village of his birth with his family, or abandon Luci to a certain death in the jungle. A silence fell over the crowd as they waited for his reply. Even the wind subsided, and the birds stopped their singing. After a long silence, Tulo spoke.

"Is there no room in your hearts for an innocent child who was born different? Are we not a people of love and compassion? Do we not share everything, our joys and sorrows? Do you truly believe that this is the work of the Shadow God, and not an accident of nature? Indeed, why would the Shadow God punish an entire village by sending this one helpless child? If it is a curse, is it not a curse on my family and me?"

Tulo faced the villagers waiting for a response, but no one spoke. However, it was painfully clear to him that the people would settle only for Luci being taken from the village and left to the elements. The witch doctor turned to Tulo, "You must decide, my chief. There are only two alternatives. I can give you some time to organize it with Sira, but they will expect your answer by first light tomorrow."

Tulo stood there for several more minutes, weighing the enormity of his decision. He walked slowly back to his hut, where Sira was waiting for him. She had heard the encounter and was waiting for him with an anxious expression. She was sad for him, realizing the weight of the decision that had just fallen on his shoulders, but she was also terrified at what she already knew in her heart would be the outcome.

He approached her slowly, hobbling, as if it were painful to walk. His shoulders were stooped, and his head low – almost to his chest. He held one hand on his forehead. His face was lined with anguish. It seemed to Sira that in that short distance from the center of the village to their hut, he had aged; he was no longer the strong, fearless warrior-hunter. With every step, the burden of his decision seemed to weigh heavier and heavier. He stopped in front of her. She waited for several long moments. Slowly, he raised his shoulders, picked up his head, and squared his jaw for what would be the most dreaded decision he had made in his life.

"My beloved Sira, this village is our birthplace; these people are our people. Our two families have lived here for generations; we have two sons born here. I, we, have a responsibility for these people. They are good and well-meaning, but they are also ignorant, the victims of the superstitions and fears that have been passed down through the ages. They need a leader; no, they need leaders – you and me. It is our destiny."

At that very moment, Sira knew he had taken his decision.

"I am sorry my beloved wife, but our Luci cannot stay. Those words pain me to my soul, but there is no other way."

Sira fell to her knees from the shock, but she had always known that this was how it was going to end. Tulo bent down to console her, but so great was her grief that she remained seemingly frozen in that position for hours. Tulo sat beside her in silence. Her two sons also came to sit beside her as well. They wrapped their arms around her and put their heads on her chest as a special sign of their love and devotion for their mother.

Tulo tucked Sira in her hammock with Luci and covered both of them with Luci's blue blanket to warm them from the chilly morning mist that had settled on the village. Her two sons slept on either side of the hammock holding her hand. Tulo looked drawn; he had not slept for the entire night. He sat alone. He knew that his decision would forever change the life of Sira, his sons and the village, but he also knew that from this moment on, he would always be alone. He could only imagine what horrible effect this would have on his beloved wife. It was her child after all. It was she who bravely bore months of discomfort, especially the pain of those last hours before Luci's birth. How would she bear the loss of this beautiful child? She was a wonderful mother, wife, and friend. The two of them were inseparable – where there was Tulo, there was Sira. What was going to become of her?

He turned to look at her. She was exhausted, sleeping fitfully. She cried softly in her sleep. Luci lay on top of her mother with her little arms wrapped around her. Despite the darkness that had settled over the village, he could hear people stirring. Today would be the first day of his new life as the cacique, the chief. He rose slowly. He ached from sitting in the same position for the night. He left the hut and walked quietly through the village, past the grand hut that would be his new home from today. He stopped alongside the river. He could barely see the opposite bank owing to the carpet of mist hanging over it. He walked several feet into the warm water and watched it form small eddies around his legs. It felt good. He saw a small log gliding down the river and watched it travel downriver, vanishing in the mist. His life, indeed, all life, was like that log. It came from somewhere up the river, traveled down the river for a short while, only to disappear in the mist. Everything had a time: a beginning, middle and an end – however long or short.

He didn't realise how long he had been standing there, nor that there was someone behind him. He was startled when the witch doctor spoke softly.

"Cacique, my chief. It is time for your decision."

"Yes, I am ready."

Both of them walked to the center of the village, where the people were slowly gathering to await his decision. The skies were dark and ominous, just as they had been for days; the mist cast an eerie, grey shadow on both men who remained standing silently. The crowd grew larger and larger. It appeared that every member of the village except Tulo's family was in attendance. There was absolute stillness as they waited… and waited…

After what seemed the longest silence, Tulo took a deep breath and addressed the villagers.

"It will be done."

Chapter 4

It Must Be Done

He then turned from the stunned crowd and walked to his hut. No one moved or spoke. He was no longer just Tulo, but now the cacique, the chief, judge and jury, and father to his tribe. He would decide the future of his people. Their fate rested in his hands, and so did the fate of Luci. *It must be done*, he thought.

He pushed down the feelings of love he felt for his daughter as he walked into his hut. To his two sons, he appeared larger, almost menacing, in his stature. They saw the expression on their father's face; it was hard and resolute. His eyes seemed cold. Instinctively, they moved away to a corner. He walked over to the hammock with the sleeping Sira and little Luci. Sira's eyes opened in time to see him leaning over her as he reached for Luci. Sira's motherly instinct took over. She held tightly on to Luci, so tightly that she stirred the baby from her sleep. Luci began to cry. *It must be done*, he continued to tell himself.

Tulo gripped Sira's wrists and pulled them apart. Sira's eyes widened in terror as she silently pleaded for Tulo to reconsider. *It must be done…*

It must be done…

Tulo's grip was no longer that of a loving husband and father. His hands felt like iron. He squeezed harder. Sira released her grip. Tulo pulled the lustrous blue blanket around Luci, who was now screaming. As he lifted her, Sira turned away from her husband, and began sobbing uncontrollably. Her baby, her dear little Luci was being sacrificed to appease some god by ignorant and superstitious people who valued their blind belief in the

Shadow God over the life of an innocent child. Tulo turned away and left the hut. *It must be done…*

He walked back to the center of the village, where the crowd was still standing motionless. He held up Luci to the group.

"I am the cacique, he who decides who lives, and who dies. As I take this child to the jungle as a sacrifice to the Shadow God, remember my words: It is I who will decide who lives, and who dies. Pray that none of you or your children must face what I am about to do, for it will be I who decides your fate." His voice was hard and cold.

For a final moment, he glared at them. It was not in the hope that they might change their minds. No, it was a final, icy reminder that this was what they wanted. This merciless act would shape him as chief and the future of the villagers. It was setting the tone for his rule. His heart was filled with anger and revulsion. He then turned and disappeared into the thick jungle foliage. Nothing would ever be the same from that moment on.

Tulo walked for hours along the worn paths, and then into the untrodden bush as he carried Luci in a makeshift backpack using her blue blanket. It was well into the night when he decided to stop. He found a nut tree, ground the fruit into a fine powder, and mixed it with honey and water that he fed Luci. Then he slept for a few hours and made his way to the spot he remembered as a young man.

As a young boy, Tulo had been left in the deep jungle as part of his initiation as a warrior. He was left without food or weapons. He had to prove himself by either living and surviving in the jungle or die. On that mission, he had found a quiet stream that ran alongside a cave where he had taken shelter during a violent storm. Whilst there, cold, hungry and wet, he prayed to Atabey, the great Mother Earth, for strength on his quest to be a warrior. It was to this spot he would take Luci.

He was tired after his daylong trek into the jungle. He held Luci in his arms to keep her warm, and soon fell into a deep sleep. But he soon awoke. He had dreamt of Sira, and for the first time since leaving the village, he allowed himself to feel, to feel the magnitude of the choice he had made: the needs of the many over the needs of Sira, Luci and his sons. Then came the pain of his choice. It washed over him like a giant wave: he had sacrificed the love of his life, Sira, for chiefdom, and was about to sacrifice the life of Luci – again, for the chiefdom. His chest heaved as he began to cry. He held little Luci even closer. He cried out, "Aneke?" (Why?) through his tears. Why was life so cruel? He was so happy then; life was so simple. He and Sira would grow old together as they watched their three children grow, who would have then had children of their own. So long as he had Sira, his life was joyous, loving – complete. He sat in the darkness and hummed a simple melody to his daughter.

Little did Tulo know that he was being watched…

In the dim, grey light of morning, Tulo set off on the last leg of his journey. He hacked his way through elephant grass, the ferns, vines and plants for an entire day until he came to the spot that he had sheltered in so long ago. Actually, he heard the spot before he saw it.

This day, there was no rain, just a thick wall of mist that shrouded the cave. He heard the gentle gurgle of the brook that signaled that the cave was just a stone's throw away.

Suddenly, he stopped, dropped to a crouch, and cocked his head. He waited, sniffing the air, and straining to hear. Did he catch the sound of footsteps? Was it an animal, or perhaps a member of a hostile tribe? In the jungle, one's sense of hearing and smell were far better than the other senses in the thick foliage; it was often the difference between life and death. His keen senses as a warrior told him that something was not right. The sounds of the jungle had stopped. The monkeys and the birds had stopped screeching and singing. Yes, there was something definitely wrong. He remained frozen in his position with Luci asleep in his backpack, and his machete wrapped tightly in his grip. He waited, sniffing the air, and listening for the slightest sound that signaled an attack. Like a panther, he could strike with lethal force in the blink of an eye.

After what felt like hours, he rose slowly, but only when he heard the familiar music of the jungle return. Whoever or whatever had retreated into the thickness of the jungle and the heavy mist. He continued on the short distance to the cave, but every few steps turned to listen and smell for any sign of an enemy. Then through the heavy mist, he saw the opening of the cave. Slowly, remaining alert, he stopped in front of the cave. The entrance resembled a mouth – the maw – of a beast ready to devour its victim. Almost immediately upon entering, Tulo was surrounded by darkness. As he walked further into the gloomy cavern, all he could hear was the fading sound of the stream at the mouth of the cave. He stopped, sat down, and was satisfied that he was out of danger. He gave Luci the remainder of the nut fruit and honey mix. He leaned against the moist wall, holding Luci in his arms, and soon fell into a deep, dreamless sleep. He awoke with a start. How long had he been asleep? For a moment, in the dim light of this cave, he forgot where he was, and what he was doing. He looked down and saw his beautiful Luci peacefully sleeping on his chest. In a flash, it came back to him. He was the cacique, the chief of his people. This was his destiny; this was Luci's destiny.

It was time. If he waited any longer, his resolve would falter. *It must be done…*

He tightly wrapped Luci in her blue blanket, and gently laid her on the ground. As he did so, he prayed. "Atabey, the great Mother of us all, what I do, I do for my people, and to appease the Shadow God. I alone am responsible for this. I beg your forgiveness; I beg this child's forgiveness. Please let her fate be quick."

Bending over, Tulo kissed Luci gently on her forehead, and then covered her entirely in the blue blanket in the vain hope that her smell would not attract the predators. He fought back the tears and heartache, turned, and left, never looking back as is the tradition of jungle warriors. Tulo walked along the stream for quite a distance, avoiding the way he took to the cave not to create what would appear to the trained eye a worn path. After two days, he arrived in the village and went directly to his hut to attend to his wife and two sons.

Vanished

Sira was gone. The two boys were huddled closely together, obviously hungry, cold and frightened. His sons could only say that they woke up several days ago to find that they were alone. Their mother had not returned. Tulo stormed into the witchdoctor's shack.

"Where is she?" he demanded angrily.

"I don't know, my chief. She has vanished."

"You will set up a search party of our best warriors. They must not return until she is found. No one in the village – no one, except the children – is permitted to eat until Sira is returned. Violate this command, and they will suffer my wrath. Summon the villagers and tell them what I have said."

"Yes, my chief."

Tulo returned to his hut, took his sons and all their possessions, and moved into the chief's hut, a large, enclosed structure with a thatched roof and wood beams which were covered in sheets of woven palm branches. Inside, there were both hammocks and a bed of animal skins. A large chair covered in fur was his throne from which he would dispense justice, decide disputes, conduct marriages, negotiate with other villages, and most importantly, ensure the equitable distribution of food. This would be his home, office and meeting room for the remainder of his life as ruler of his tribe.

After feeding his sons, he walked through the village, but it seemed to the villagers that it was more like the prowling of a jungle panther. Everyone who saw him retreated into their huts, so great was the fear he evoked. His gaze full of fury, he carried his machete in his hand.

To the villagers, Tulo had now become more than their tribal chief; he had become a bitter and ruthless warder. For Tulo, this was the price the villagers would pay for the ignorance and cruelty shown to him and his beloved Sira.

It was they who demanded that Luci be abandoned to the Shadow God as a condition of his chiefdom. However, the darkness, rain and thunder had not stopped as the villagers expected. The curse of the Shadow God had not been lifted. In fact, the weather had become worse. Indeed, more rain was falling; the nearby river was overflowing its banks and threatened to engulf the village. Food was washed away, and animals and people continued disappearing into the jungle. Had they misread the signs? Had the people of the village made a tragic mistake? It was they who demanded that Luci be sacrificed in the hope that the Shadow God would lift this curse, and as a condition of Tulo becoming chief. Tulo had fulfilled his commitment, but conditions had become worse.

It was late one evening when the group of warriors sent to look for Sira returned, beaten and sullen. They were bloodied; some had been lost in battle.

The group leader approached Tulo and fell to one knee. "My chief, we searched for five days. There was no trace of our beloved Sira anywhere. We went to several villages to enquire, but no one had seen her. In the course of our search, we were ambushed by the Sawalis. We were outnumbered four to one. We lost three of our best warriors who fought bravely. I am sorry, my chief. You must know that we tried."

Tulo nodded. He thought for a long time. *Should I continue to punish these warriors? I know that they tried. And how much longer can I punish the women and old men of the village? They had only consumed water for the past several days, as he had commanded. How much longer?* The group of warriors waited on bended knees for the punishment they expected from this heartless chief for failure to find Sira.

Tulo closed his eyes, and heaved a deep sigh, but to their surprise "Go. Be with your families. Tell everyone in the village that they may now eat." He turned and walked away.

As he sat alone in the dim light of the hut, he replayed all the events leading up to abandoning Luci. He then remembered the incident in the jungle when it had fallen silent. He thought, why did the birds and monkeys fall silent? Such would only happen only when they perceived a threat or something unusual. Suddenly, the thought came to him. Could it have been her? Is it possible…? She is a clever, determined woman who, like him, knew the jungle intimately. They had played there as children. She could have easily become one of the warriors. Only she would have attempted it. He whispered, "Sira, my beloved Sira, what have you done? Where are you?"

Chapter 6

A Mother's Pain

Sira knew that the jungle had given her away as soon as the monkeys and birds stopped screeching and singing. Surely, Tulo would know that he was being followed. She dropped to the ground, and quickly covered herself with grass, palm leaves, and wild orchids to mask her scent. She slowed her breathing and remained perfectly still for the greater part of the day, until she fell fast asleep. The chorus of monkeys and birds awakened her. However, she decided to remain hidden under the branches and leaves for another day in the event that Tulo returned along this way. She had only eaten berries, and had taken water from several plants, but neither hunger nor lack of sleep would deter her. It was the driving force for her to risk everything. She would find Luci, her beautiful Luci. After that, she would put her faith in Atabey, the Great Earth Mother.

After two days of lying under cover, she rose slowly and painfully. She took measured steps, mindful that Tulo might still be crouched in the bush, waiting to attack his stalker. It took nearly another whole day for her to reach the stream. She walked along the bank until she came upon the opening of a cave. Yes, she thought, this is where he would have taken Luci. She ran into the entrance without giving thought to what might have been lurking inside. *Luci, my Luci, where are you?* She felt the walls, crawled on her hands, scraping her knees, searching every corner. She listened for the cry of a cold and hungry baby, but there was only silence and Luci's blue blanket. With a heart that was breaking, she called out, "Luci, my Luci, where are you?" In reply, she only heard the echo of her voice. She fell to her knees and sobbed.

Luci was gone.

Sira sat for a long time in the darkness. She had come to the realisation that her beloved child had been taken, probably by the predators who sheltered in the cave to feast on their prey. However, it suddenly struck her that something was odd: there was no evidence of violence. Wouldn't there be other horrific signs of a predator? But there was nothing. All that was left was the blue blanket that Tulo had wrapped her in. Maybe, just maybe, someone from another village had found her? No, that couldn't be. She was different: white skin, silky blonde hair and blue eyes. No other villager would have dared touch her for fear of a curse.

The pieces of the puzzle did not fit. There was – there had to be – another explanation. Sira got up, picked up the blue blanket and clutched it to her chest. Even under the smell of dampness, she could still detect the scent of her baby. She walked into the jungle, now more determined than ever to find her beloved Luci – never to be seen again.

Chapter 7

A Broken Heart

Tulo sent search party after search party in search of his beloved Sira. He sent emissaries to the nearby villages to enquire about her whereabouts. He offered rewards. After months of searching, Tulo, the cacique, the chief, resigned himself that he had lost both a daughter and his beloved wife. Despite the offering of regrets by the villagers for his loss, Tulo could not be consoled. He remained alone in the tribal grand hut. He rarely participated in village affairs, and ceremonies. He spoke only to the witchdoctor to communicate with the outside. His sons were sent to live with their grandparents. Tulo had cut himself off from the world.

His bitterness and loneliness consumed him. His heart burned with anger for the very people in the village whom he had sworn to protect. Secretly, he hated them. He only found peace in the darkness and isolation of his grand hut – alone.

And so, it was for years that Tulo, the cacique, lived in solitude, loneliness and bitterness. One morning, the villagers arose, and to their amazement, the curse of the Shadow God had disappeared. The sun shone through the high trees; the rain had stopped, and life was returning to normal. After all this time, had the Shadow God been appeased by the sacrifice of the little girl? Or was it something else? Could it be Sira who interceded with the Shadow God to lift the curse? No one would ever know. One morning, as the mist gave way to the heat of the sun, his sons, now grown, found their father. He was clutching one of Sira's dresses. It was said that he had died of a broken heart.

Tulo's elder son, Tulim, became chief, the cacique. The village prospered and grew to be the largest in the jungle. The tragedy of Tulo, Sira and little Luci faded into history and became just a legend. For the village, that was the end of the story.

But little did they know, it was only the beginning....

Chapter 8

Capuchin Monkeys and Treetops

She lay there quietly at first, but then hunger, and the lack of warmth from her mother overtook her. What first began as crying turned into angry screams. Her arms and legs flailed, which only served to push the blue blanket away. Now, she was both hungry and cold, and very frightened in the darkness of the cave. No one had come to feed her, hold her, and speak softly to reassure her. She was alone.

The unusual screaming drew the attention of the Capuchin monkeys. Capuchin monkeys are small creatures about the same size as baby Luci. Their faces were white, their body fur was white in front and a light brown mixed with black on their backs and legs. Curious by nature, the troop climbed down from the safety of their treetop lofts to inspect the source of the unusual noise. They cautiously walked into the cave led by the alpha male and alpha female both of whom were larger and more aggressive than the other monkeys. They slowly approached baby Luci. They instinctively knew she was not a threat, and quickly realised that she was very different from monkeys in many ways. No, she was not a monkey, nor was she like the humans they had seen in the forest. The alpha female cautiously approached the baby, who immediately raised her arms to be held. The monkey gently picked up this unusual little creature who immediately put her arms around the warm body of the female Capuchin. With her maternal instinct aroused, she pressed the little baby to her chest. Luci stopped crying instantly and began cooing.

The male Capuchin was not as agreeable, however. Although he knew instinctively that this creature was different, he was also concerned that this infant might be a threat to his troop. He grunted and snorted his disapproval. However, the female monkey did not share his misgivings. The alpha male knew better than to make an issue of it with her. The other female monkeys in the troop approached the baby, gently touching the soft body and feeling her unusual skin and hair. They took turns in passing the infant around, and soon began petting the little creature, and making affectionate, cooing sounds. The alpha female, who could no longer have children of her own owing to her advanced years, took little Luci as her own. Baby monkeys know instinctively from birth to grasp their mother's neck. The mother would then climb into the trees for safety, but baby Luci did not have that skill or instinct being a human. Holding the baby with one arm, Luci's now adopted monkey-mother made her way high into the trees. She put her new baby in the crook of tree branches and went off to find soft fruit to feed her.

Luci had now also disappeared. The only evidence of her life was her blue blanket left behind in the cave.

And so, the lush jungle treetops became Luci's first home. She was surrounded day and night by the troop of monkeys who served as her nurses, providers, and protectors. Her early days passed peacefully. Given her unusual nature, the female monkeys who had taken turns looking after her or, more accurately, guarding her were terrified after one frightening incident. Whereas baby monkeys can hold on to their mothers while they sleep, Luci tossed and turned when she was asleep. One morning, as the alpha female was returning with a handful of fruit, to her horror, Luci was nowhere to be found! She had rolled out of her nest and had fallen down several branches; she was saved only by the thick foliage at the treetops. Luci was screaming, making it easier for the alpha female to find her. She suffered several bruises, but after some food and a cuddle from the female monkey, she quieted down, and was soon fast asleep. From that point on, the female monkeys organized themselves into a round-the-clock guard to ensure that Luci remained in her safe place. But, as this baby grew, she began to crawl. Thus, keeping her in the tree became a daily challenge. The monkey "on duty" had the job of stopping this human baby from crawling along the branch, unaware of the danger of falling. She might not be so fortunate the next time she fell.

Chapter 9

Of Jaguars and Fairies

It soon became obvious that Luci was outgrowing her treetop home. One day, as the troop of monkeys prepared to move to another area of the forest, the alpha female monkey took Luci down to the ground, aware that this child could not swing from the trees like the other monkey children or hang on to her while she swung from vine to vine. As Luci was now almost as large as the monkeys themselves, the alpha monkey struggled to get her down to the jungle floor. Luci's monkey-mother half carried, and half dragged her to the new tree, carefully avoiding the dangers lurking on the ground. However, when the alpha female tried to climb to their new home, she quickly realised that Luci was now too large and too heavy to lift. Unlike the other young monkeys, Baby Luci did not understand that she was supposed to hold on to her mother as she climbed up the tree. Moreover, Luci had just discovered on her brief contact with the jungle floor that she could happily crawl in any direction on a flat surface. Her monkey-mother tried desperately to stop her, but every attempt was met with Luci's loudly protesting at the attempt to restrain her.

The howling of the baby did not go unnoticed in the jungle…

The scent and the sound had alerted a nearby hungry jaguar, a fast, short-distance runner. It quickly began its stealthy and patient stalk of what it realised was prey. The monkeys sensed the lurking danger, and immediately made for the treetops amid screeches to alert the other members of the troop, leaving only Luci, and monkey-mother at ground level. Luci was excited at her ability to crawl freely, and had even attempted, albeit unsuccessfully, to stand up. The mother monkey smelled the jungle cat and saw it hiding in the brush. The piercing cold yellow eyes of the predator told the mother monkey that it was about to strike. She realised that she had a fateful choice: Try to fend off a jaguar which could weigh up to 220 pounds – a battle that she instinctively knew she could not win; or save herself and flee up into the safety of the treetop canopy. Her survival instincts took over, and screeching in anger, the alpha monkey took to the trees.

Luci was now alone and completely unaware of the danger.

Owing to the thick jungle canopy, daylight faded quickly on the jungle floor. That suited the big cat that maintained its hidden position, patiently waiting for right moment to strike the strange creature crawling on the ground. As the light continued to fade, the predator moved closer to its quarry, ever so slowly, totally focused on the kill. Each step of the large cat was measured, and silent.

Closer…

From the treetops, the of troop monkeys screeched in fear and warning. The alpha female could only watch helplessly. Luci kept crawling, enjoying her newfound freedom of movement, but heedless of the imminent danger.

Closer…

The jaguar tensed his muscles, ready to lunge. Now! The jaguar sprang forward with tremendous force, growling, his fangs bared ready for the kill. But the next instant, to the cat's amazement, a ball of light burst in front of him. Suddenly, the jungle floor was bathed in dazzling white light, bright as the noonday sun. At that moment, the large ball broke into hundreds of pieces to reveal tiny fairies enclosed in their own light bubbles. Half of them surrounded the jaguar; the rest encircled the little baby. Startled, the jaguar fled into the bushes; Luci gurgled happily and kept trying to grab these floating balls of light.

The fairies were delicate little creatures with fluttering wings. Although they resembled little children, they were really ageless. Their laughter sounded like tinkling bells. They surrounded Luci, and then magically rejoined themselves into one large bubble of light. Now in the cocoon of light, Luci felt warm and secure. As quickly as the flash of light had appeared, it vanished along with Luci.

Chapter 10

The Fairy Queen

In the next instant, the ball of light carrying Luci, reappeared in a part of the jungle that no one, not even the local tribes, would dare venture into. It was even denser than any other part of the landscape. The sun never penetrated the treetop there. It was said to be haunted by ghosts resembling old men and women in rags. The elders said that if a member of the tribe looked into the eyes of these spirits, they would go mad, and never be seen again. Others said that this place was infested with little flying creatures resembling sweet, laughing children who were really daughters of the evil Shadow God in disguise. They would lie in wait for an unsuspecting tribal member, and then with a sting, would turn them into stone.

Of course, none of the stories were true. However, it did serve the purposes of the Fairy Queen and her flock of fairies. They lived in quiet harmony with all the creatures of the jungle, the flowers, the shrubs and the trees. The fairies could speak to all the animals and protect them from intruders. They tended the flowers, the fruits, and all the trees. This part of the deep jungle was truly a green paradise – untouched by man. Each fairy was named after a flower, fruit or tree. They lived among the trees with leaves which served both as shelter from the rain, and a bed at night.

It was here that the ball of light reappeared. The Fairy Queen was waiting for them. Her name was Mab. The queen of the fairies was larger and older than the troop. In fact, she was ageless. She was beautiful, wise, and the most powerful of all the fairies. Her hair was the colour of gold, and the strands of hair floated around her head like an aura. She wore a brilliant white dress that shimmered, and a long blue stole over her shoulders. She also possessed the most powerful magic. Ever so gently, the fairies laid Luci before her. The queen took Luci in her arms.

"Well, well, little one. You gave us a scare, but you are safe now. We know all that you have been through, and at such a tender age. What is to become of you? Surely, we cannot send you back to your village. You cannot live in the jungle with monkeys. The queen of the monkeys, Kerwani, told us of your plight, and your near-death experience with our friend, Kisha, the jaguar."

Queen Mab closed her eyes; she held baby Luci for many long moments, deep in thought. Then, opening her eyes, she called, "Gather around, my children, I want you to hear my decision." In an instant, thousands of tiny balls of light descended from the treetops, the air, and the many flowers that dotted the jungle floor. There was Daisy Fairy, Rose Fairy, Tulip Fairy, Honeysuckle Fairy, Lilly Fairy, and many, many more. Their fluttering wings felt like a soft breeze; and their gentle laughter sounded like bells; their collective voices resembled the buzz of a honeybee.

"This poor child has no home. She has been abandoned because of ignorance and fear. We cannot allow her to be a victim. Therefore, I have decided that we will adopt Luci. We will raise her, protect her, feed her and teach her. Each and every one of you will have a part to play in helping this child grow to be healthy, strong, and independent. She will no longer be without a family. From now on, she will be a part of our family. We will teach her the ways of the fairies, and the way of humans. She will become a very special person – unlike any other of human kind."

Chapter 11

The Early Years – Tumbles and Fun

And so, the days and years passed peacefully. Luci grew with each day, surrounded by fairies who clothed and washed her with warm rainwater, fed her the fruits of the jungle, played with her, and generally watched over her every move. But not every day was so happy for either Luci or the fairies. There was the time when she stumbled trying her first steps and fell face down into the jungle mud. Luci howled and could not be consoled despite all the best efforts of the fairies to wash her and comfort her. From that moment on, Luci's every attempt to walk was met with many of the fairies holding her hands and arms, encouraging her, and giggling with her every shaky step.

One day, Luci decided to stop crawling and rise to her feet. Immediately, she was surrounded by numerous fairies that were ready to hold her hand, but this time she shook them off. Luci was walking! The fairies floated close by in the event that she stumbled again. It wasn't necessary. She walked, and even tried to reach out to catch a butterfly. For Luci, it was the beginning of her adventure. However, for the fairies, it was the beginning of a constant chase to keep up with her – to ensure that she didn't wander too far, or, worse come to harm in the often cruel jungle. It was always assumed that as spirits of the forest, fairies never got tired, but Luci quickly disproved that theory. As Luci fell off to sleep at the end of each day, the exhausted fairies did the same. Raising a child, they discovered, was indeed hard work!

Most children had toys, games, and building blocks. Not Luci. Instead, she had an extraordinary playground: the forest, its flowers, trees and animals that served to amuse and entertain her, and of course, the ever-present fairies as companions with whom she played endless games. The fairies were not only her friends and guardians, they were also her teachers.

Daisy Fairy taught her to read; Rose Fairy taught her to run, swim, jump, and climb trees. And, Tulip Fairy taught her the nutritional plants and flowers she could eat, and how to prepare the food. From Lily Fairy she learned the ways of the forest, particularly, the animals that made the jungle both beautiful, and at the same time dangerous. Lemon Fairy taught Luci mathematics.

Every day, Luci would take walks with many of the fairies flitting around her teaching her to sing, whistle and chirp like the birds. But it was Mab, the Queen of all the Fairies, who taught her perhaps the most important lesson: to speak – in several languages and how to communicate with the animals, the trees and the plants.

Queen Mab was teaching Luci how to become a fairy.

Chapter 12

Mam Daear

Today was a special day for fairies all over the world. At sunrise, the flower fairies, the water fairies, the tree fairies – all watched in silence and awe as the first rays of the sun broke over the hillside. It was the feast of Mam Daear – the celebration of Mother Earth. For fairies, all of whom are descended from Mother Earth, this was indeed a day to celebrate. They were excited and had been preparing for weeks for this event. They strung hundreds of bell-shaped flowers: Lily of the Valley, Mountain Heather, and Snow Drops from the branches of trees. They prepared a feast of milk, morning dew, honey, berries of all kinds, sweet butter and honey cakes.

A special table was prepared for Luci and Mab. This was a day to sing and dance. Some fairies played the flute; others played bells, trumpets, and harps. Other fairies formed a chorus and sang ancient songs. Hundreds, perhaps thousands of fairy circles spun around the treetops. It was a glorious day, a day that was special for Luci. She was growing up as part of a family – albeit a unique one. Luci, now seven years old, turned to Mab, and with a heart bursting with happiness said, "Mother, I want this day to last forever."

Chapter 13

Kerwani and The Library Adventure

Months grew into years, and each successive year saw the young girl grow to be an intelligent, beautiful and very capable young woman. She and the fairies built a "bohea", a lean-to of palm leaves and bamboo. Strung across the bohea was a hammock; and, in the corner, a table. The fairies kept a constant supply of honeysuckle that they hung throughout the hut, and that gave the air a sweet fragrance. Her clothes were made of delicate corn silk woven by the fairies. When she ran, her clothes seemed to float around her.

Luci was athletic; she could climb up to the treetops and sit with the monkeys. She especially enjoyed her time with Kerwani, the Queen of the Monkeys. They would spend afternoons in thoughtful conversation. Luci was learning to grunt, screech, and sometimes bark when there was danger. Kerwani would laugh heartily at Luci's attempts at monkey speak.

"My dear Luci, good try. I think I understand, but what you actually said was, 'your thumb is in my nose.'"

A part of every day in Luci's life was devoted to learning. She spent hours with Queen Mab and the other fairies. She was a quick learner, and particularly enjoyed her language and history lessons. Among their lesser qualities, fairies could be very mischievous. Sometimes, the fairies would visit a library in a faraway city at night to "borrow" a book Luci needed for her studies. With the benefit of the books and the lessons from each of her teacher fairies, Luci has "acquired" a library of her own.

On their first visit to a library in the nearby village of Humaita in search of language books, the fairies returned with 240 books on the world's most popular languages. They had emptied the library of every language book! As each fairy arrived with book after book, the piles grew higher and higher to the point where there wasn't much room for anything else in her hut. Luci was thrilled, but Queen Mab was more restrained. "My dear children, I commend you on your enthusiasm, but I asked for several books, not the entire library."

Peach Fairy replied, "We are sorry, Mother, but we weren't certain of the languages you wanted. So, we took them all." There was a twitter of laughter from the other fairies.

"You are quite right. I will decide which languages we will teach Luci. You can return the rest."

On the first morning, one can only imagine the shock of the librarian when she discovered that her entire inventory of language books had disappeared. She was even more baffled when all but six books were back on the shelves the following morning, neatly arranged in the correct order.

Chapter 14

Kisha – A Forever Friend

Luci had become good friends with Kisha, the jaguar who, years ago, saw Luci as a possible meal. Kisha was now much older. He came over to Luci and acknowledged the young woman by rubbing his face against Luci's cheek – a sign of friendship. In return, Luci put her hand on Kisha's face and gently petted him. The old jaguar made purring, throaty and guttural sounds much like a house cat.

"Well, my dear friend, are you up to a little run today? Your old bones could use some exercise."

"Ah, so you think you can outrun me, a jaguar, the fastest and fiercest member of this forest?"

"No, but it would be worth the try."

"All right then, let's go!" With that, Kisha bounded up, and ran into the jungle.

"Wait, Kisha. I didn't want to race – just have a jog."

As fast as the jaguar had disappeared, it came bounding out of the thick foliage. "Oh, okay. For a moment there, I thought you were challenging me."

"No, my friend. I could never outrun you, but I did get you up on your feet!"

"You are a naughty girl, Luci, trying to outsmart me," came Kisha's deep-throated response.

Luci laughed. "Okay, why don't we just take a stroll?"

Kisha grumbled as they walked along the path to a small clearing with the fairies close behind. Luci was too preoccupied with dancing among the wildflowers with the fairies to be alert to any danger. It was too late before the fairies noticed, but there was an impending danger to Luci's life. The jaguar raced toward her in a flash, roaring as he went. The young girl turned to see the big cat bearing down on her with a ferocious roar and fangs bared. She was terrified that she was the object of his ferocity for a moment, but Kisha flashed past her like a blur. At the very instant, Razza, the hooded cobra was about to strike Luci, Kisha attacked the snake instead. Knowing it was a battle she could not win, Razza retreated, but not before inflicting a bite on Kisha. The snake's venom being deadly, reacted quickly and Kisha collapsed after taking only a few trembling steps.

The fairies, true to their duty, surrounded Luci who was terrified by the sight of the deadly snake, and overwhelmed with fear for her friend, Kisha who was now lying on the ground motionless. Several of the fairies immediately made a tourniquet from reeds and wrapped it around Kisha's leg. Hopefully, that would stop the deadly poison from spreading. Kisha's breaths came slowly.

Luci looked to her fairies and pleaded, "Please, my sisters, please take her to Queen Mab. She is the only one who can cure our friend, Kisha." The fairies came together and formed a brilliant bubble of light. They gently lifted Kisha and floated away with Luci running alongside.

The fairies laid Kisha at the feet of the Queen. With a wave of her hand, Kisha's limp body slowly rose, lifted by an unseen force. The Queen placed her hand on the jaguar, closed her eyes, and began a low hum. What began as two notes, low then high, grew into a beautiful melody, like a chorus of birds at first light in the morning. She then lowered Kisha, who was now breathing steadily.

"My child," the Queen said as she turned to Luci. "Now, we must wait. All will be well." Luci rushed over to the large cat and petted his face.

"Mother, he saved my life."

"Yes, I know. Your sisters told me. It was not only an act of heroism, but also an act of friendship, indeed, one of love."

After a moment of silence, Queen Mab put a hand on Luci's shoulder, sensing the girl's feelings, and said gently, "You must not be angry with Razza. Like so many of the creatures of the rain forest, she acted according to her nature. She meant no harm; she was protecting her eggs."

"But, Mother, if Kisha had not intervened, Razza would have bitten me."

"Yes, my child, she would have, but there is a lesson here for you. The mother of us all, the Great Earth Mother, created all the creatures of the jungle to follow their nature, their instincts. There are no good or bad animals. Perhaps, one day, you will learn to live alongside all living beings in harmony, without fear or judgment."

"Yes, Mother, I will try," Luci replied. She sat beside Kisha and did not move from his side. She awoke the next morning to find Kisha lying beside her with his eyes wide open, staring at her. She gave the big cat a hug.

"I'm so happy to see that you are feeling better, Kisha. Thank you, thank you for saving me."

Kisha rose unsteadily to his feet and put his face against Luci's in an expression of love. In his characteristic throaty rumble, he said, "Next time, please try not to aggravate the likes of Razza, and her slithery friends. These bones are getting a bit too old for rescuing fairies." He winked at Luci, and limped away into the dense foliage, grumbling about having gone a whole day without a morsel of food.

Chapter 15

Who Am I?

Luci was now fluent in several languages. She studied world history, the history of the native people who lived in the rainforest, mathematics and science. She could now converse with her teacher fairies on various subjects and displayed a quick wit and a keen mind. She loved learning. She was also a natural athlete. She swam with the water fairies; climbed with the tree fairies; and ran like the wind with the flower fairies (avoiding, of course, Razza's hole, and those of her family!)

One evening, she was sitting quietly with Queen Mab and her sister fairies, enjoying the cool air and the sweet music of birds, frogs, crickets and the numerous other sounds from the jungle world around them. Luci, who was now thirteen, looked puzzled as she turned to the Fairy Queen.

"Mother."

"Yes, my child. What is it?"

Luci tightened her lips and narrowed her eyes. "Mother, I know that I'm not like my sisters, or for that matter, like you. I know that I am not a monkey." She hesitated for a moment, and then said, "Are there others like me?"

Mab smiled gently. "Yes, dear, there are many, many others. They are called 'human beings or 'people'. Perhaps, not as many as there are fairies, and the spirits, but no, you are not alone."

Luci was now confused. "If that is so, why have I never seen them?"

Mab was silent for several long moments. The fairies fell silent. It appeared as if the entire forest had gone silent.

The Queen of the Fairies began, slowly, "I think that you are old enough now to learn who you are, and where you came from." At that, the Queen began. She told Luci of her birth to her parents, Tulo and Sira, members of an Arawak tribe in the remote jungle of the Amazon Rain Forest. She went on to tell the young girl that when she was born, her skin was the palest white, and her hair was as yellow as corn silk, but her parents and the tribe were much darker skinned with dark straight hair. The tribe considered Luci to have been a curse brought down by the Shadow God. They demanded that to lift a curse, the little baby should be abandoned. Her father, who was now the chief of the tribe, consented with a heavy heart. Her mother, Sira, was devastated, but could do nothing to convince her husband to reject the tribe's demands.

"Your father took you to a cave by a nearby river and left you there. Unknown to your father, your mother followed him to rescue you, but you were gone by the time she got to the cave. So overwhelmed was your mother at the loss of her beautiful Luci that she entered the forest and was never seen again. Your father, who had now lost both his beloved daughter and wife, died of a broken heart later. It is a sad and tragic tale of ignorance, prejudice and the fear of what is different. But, at the same time, it is a tale of love, love of a mother and father. I am so sorry to tell you these things, my dear Luci."

"But how did I get here?"

"You were first rescued by the Alpha Female, Kerwani, whom you know, and then by us from a certain jaguar, named Kisha, whom you also know."

"Kisha wanted to eat me?!"

"I'm afraid so. Remember, he was acting not from evil intention, but only from his nature as a hunter. Then, we saved you from Kisha who now regrets his earlier desire to eat you. You mustn't be angry with him."

"Hmm, he really wanted to eat me?" She still couldn't believe it.

Mab raised her eyebrows, cocked her head, and nodded with a crooked smile.

Luci was a strong-willed person, much like her father. She would pursue this until she got all her questions answered. The queen did answer all of her questions without hesitation, without withholding any details.

A deep sadness came over Luci. Her father had died; her mother had disappeared. For as much as she loved the Queen Mother and her sister fairies, she could not help but feel her parents' loss. This would be one of Luci's first life lessons: life was not always like it was here in the world of the fairies; it could be cruel and pitiless.

Chapter 16

Humans and People

"One last question, Mother. How is it that I have never seen any of these human beings, these people? Where are they?"

"Although fairies and spirits are everywhere, we live in the most remote part of the rainforest. No one would dare to come anywhere near here as we have created a tale that anyone who ventures here would be cursed and turned to stone or worse."

Luci persisted. "May I see where I was born, Mother?"

"That would not be a good idea, my child. If they were to see you, there would be fear and panic. They would see only that the cursed child had returned to haunt them, to bring down the anger of the Shadow God." The Queen was silent for a few moments, then continued, "However, I do think we could show you other people."

Luci was thrilled. She would see people – just like her...well, almost. Although she had never seen other people, she did know that she was different in some ways. Seeing other people would help her understand so much.

As if reading her mind, the Fairy Queen said, "Luci, it is true that people are the same in many ways, but they are also very different from each other."

Now, Luci was really confused. "But, Mother, you just said..."

"I said that they are human beings; and that you are not alone. Just as there are many varieties of flowers and butterflies, there are many varieties of human beings.

Like flowers and butterflies, they come in various colors, shapes, and sizes. They come from places all over the world. The majority of people live in communities – large and small, each having different roles, like flowers and butterflies. And, like the people from the little village where you were born, each of these villages has different cultures, values and beliefs. Too often, these communities, and the people within the village, are in conflict with one another, often with tragic consequences. Do you understand, Luci?"

"I think so," she said almost in a whisper. "But why, why is there conflict? Why can't it be like it is here?"

Mab felt a pang of sorrow for this young, innocent girl. How could she tell her about the world outside the jungle, a world in turmoil and fear, war, famine, and prejudice? "For all my years, I too have asked the same questions. I have concluded that there is no one answer. Often, it is power, greed, or the absence of love and compassion for other members of the community, especially those who are different in some way – much like you, and the helpless and the poor. In some instances, it is a desire of one group of people, or even individuals, to dominate others. People fear what they do not know. Your sister fairies and I wanted to protect you from all that. I see now that it was my mistake. You deserve to see both sides of the leaf: the one that drinks in the sun and thrives in loving harmony with Mother Nature; and the other side of the leaf that lives in the darkness."

With the leaf in her mind, Luci asked, "But, it is the same leaf, is it not?"

"Yes, my dear, Luci, and that is what makes human beings – people – so difficult to understand, unlike the animals of our forest world that act according to their natures, like Razza, or the monkeys, and even Kisha. People, on the other hand, often act in strange and contradictory ways. They are often capable of great acts of love and kindness, and at the same time, equally capable of horrific acts of hatred and inhumanity. They can display uncommon and spontaneous acts of generosity and compassion for others, and then turn around with acts of unspeakable cruelty."

There was a long silence.

Queen Mab spoke with a mixture of sadness and resignation. "We shall go to the edge of the forest so that you may see others like you.

Chapter 17

The Happy March… Almost

The next day, Mab assembled a large group of fairies to accompany her and Luci to the edge of the forest. Within moments, all the fairies in the forest knew of the expedition. The tree fairies, the flower fairies, and the water and fruit fairies were preparing a safe path to the edge. They spoke to all the animals to give Luci and the Fairy Mother safe passage. As they started their journey, they were joined by the troop of monkeys who leaped from tree to tree, led by Kerwani, the alpha female. Kisha strolled over and asked to join the travelers.

"Did you *really* try to eat me?" Luci asked the old jaguar.

"Luci, remember what I said," came the firm voice from her fairy Mother.

"Yes, I do remember, but, Mother, he tried to eat me!!"

Kisha walked over to Luci, and said in his most contrite voice, "Well, Luci, I was young and foolish then. Besides, I had never tasted a human before, and I thought…. Well, the truth is I don't think I would have eaten you. You were so small. Probably, not enough to fill my belly."

"Mother!" Luci called out.

Mab and the other fairies were laughing at Kisha's stumbling effort at asking for forgiveness.

"Okay, okay, I'm sorry, Luci," the jaguar said. He turned away, and then said almost in a whisper, "And, I'm not sure about the taste…." Of course, the fairies and Mab heard it and laughed all the harder.

The group walked through the forest in a single file under a canopy of trees along a path that the fairies had prepared. It was an unusual sight in the jungle: hundreds of fairies flying around, giggling, and playing. The monkeys were swinging through the trees, screeching happily. Kisha lumbered along while grumbling about his empty belly. Mab, the Fairy Queen, spoke about all the breathtaking features in the forest. She pointed to the beautiful flowers: the white and purple orchids, cacao, passion fruit, and lilies. She stopped occasionally to speak to the birds, lizards, sloths, and macaws. Beautiful butterflies with dazzling colors flew in zigzags around Luci. Luci held Queen Mab's hand and was chattering gaily. She was so excited about the prospect of seeing the edge of the jungle and "people" like her.

"Mother, do the 'people' really look like me?"

"Yes, my child," she replied with sadness in her voice, "Yes, they do look like you, but not as beautiful."

The march continued for the greater part of the day. Luci suddenly stopped. She held her head up to sniff the air. Something was wrong. The sweet fragrance of the jungle had changed. It was a strange and unpleasant odor. Mab, and the fairies knew; Kisha, and the monkeys knew what that pungent odor was.

Smoke.

Luci turned to the Queen Mother with a quizzical look. "Mother?"

The Queen spoke softly, "My dear, Luci, it is called smoke, smoke from the burning of the trees."

"Burning? Trees? But why? Why would anyone burn a tree?"

Mab did not respond to the question. "Come, child, let me show you."

After a short walk, the group stopped. In the distance, they could see an open field covered in a thick, choking smoke from an enormous fire that reached high into the sky, nearly blotting out the sun. The blaze was consuming the jungle trees that had been cut down and piled in a mountainous heap. All that remained were the charred stumps of thousands of trees where once there were majestic palm and banana trees, millions of flowers, shrubs and vines. A moderate breeze rose, pushing the thick smoke away to reveal the remains of many jungle animals that could not escape the inferno. Large machines plowing up the stumps and burned grasses at the other end of the charred field, pushing them into large mounds. Behind these machines were even larger ones that turned the field into neatly aligned rows ready for planting. They raised swirling clouds of dust in their wake. The roar from these machine monsters was deafening.

Riding on the machines and walking in the fields were several hundred "people". They were dressed in dusty, grimy clothes, yellow helmets and orange vests. They moved slowly in the heat of the Amazon sun. Queen Mab explained that these "people" were part of an effort by the government to convert more of the rain forest into cornfields and grazing land to feed the hungry "people" of Brazil and the world.

Luci was stunned, and at the same time, struck by the sight of other humans who vaguely looked like her. A thousand thoughts were flying through her head. *Yes, they look like me, sort of. But why are they doing this? So many innocent animals were killed. So many of the tree spirits were lost.* The tree fairies cried. The deafening roar of all these machines overwhelmed her. She covered her ears.

Chapter 18

The Encounter

Suddenly, a strange-looking vehicle came speeding toward them. Evidently, the "people" had seen a young girl, a jaguar and a troop of monkeys standing in the distance. Luci had never seen such a thing before; she could not take her eyes away from this weird object – a truck. Kisha uttered a low growl and bared his teeth; the monkeys started to screech in alarm.

Humans could not see or hear fairies or the forest spirits. So, to the approaching humans, Luci was standing alone at the jungle's edge. Luci was so hypnotized by what was unfolding before her eyes, and what sounded like rolling thunder from this incredible thing that she didn't hear the Queen of the Fairies say to her, "Be careful, child. Although they look like you, they are not like you."

The truck stopped not ten feet in front of Luci. A dozen gruff-looking men carrying long metal sticks poured out from the inside of this beast. They ran toward the little girl and surrounded her. She was now so afraid that she felt frozen to the spot.

"Who are you?" shouted a large "human" with his big stick. He was tall, fat and had a scruffy beard. His clothes were dirty; his belly hung over a belt that had what Luci thought were shiny metal beads. The large man approached cautiously. He saw the jaguar, teeth bared, growling, and a large troop of monkeys looking very menacingly at the man. He stopped and assessed his chances of getting any closer to this beautiful girl with long blonde hair and skin pale as goat milk. Kisha lowered his head and crouched down, getting ready to pounce; the monkeys began encircling the men. The man raised the long stick in the air. It then exploded with a boom, flame shooting outside one end. Kisha shrank back, and the monkeys scattered into the trees.

Still, the ugly-looking man with the stick that spit fire did not get any closer. He thought to himself, *is she real or is it a ghost? Perhaps, an evil spirit to punish us.* He had heard of the dark spirits that inhabited the jungle, and the tales of people who were turned to stone by those spirits. Turning to the other men in his group, the gruff-looking leader sneered, "What do you think, boys? She doesn't look like an evil spirit to me, eh, just a lost girl. She should fetch a good sum at the slave market." The men were eyeing the beautiful girl, but still leery of getting any closer mindful of the legend of the dark spirits.

The fat leader decided to take his chances. He took a step forward. He had an evil smile that showed brown stained teeth. And when he spoke, he spit through his beard. He tried to sound soothing, but his voice came across more as a snake's hiss, "Well, pretty girl, what are you doing here, so far away from the village? Are you lost? Why don't you come with us? We'll take you back."

She heard the distress in the Queen's voice, "My child, run back into the forest! They mean to take you!" Luci took a step back and turned, but the burly man rushed toward her before she could run.

At the same instant, Kisha reappeared from the jungle, with fangs bared and a blood-curdling roar, and lunged at the man. He swung his fire stick at the jaguar, who fell to the ground with a yelp. Luci rushed over to him, but the large cat was unconscious.

For the first time in her life, Luci was overcome with a new, and strange feeling. Her face was red, her eyes bulged, and her hands were balled into fists. Her heart was racing, and she felt sick at this terrible feeling. Anger, rage swelled up as she shouted, "What have you done? Why are you doing this?"

The leader called out, "Take her!" One of the men ran over to Luci, and grabbed her arm, pulling her toward the monster vehicle. His grip was hard and rough. Luci could smell the ugly man's harsh breath and rancid body as he reached for her. She tried to pull away, and as she did so, he slapped her so hard that she fell to the ground hitting her head on the monster vehicle. For a moment, she felt the world spinning around her. She had a coppery taste in her mouth from the blood that was running down her face from the gash on her head. The man continued to drag her by her hair toward the truck, and in the process, ripped her white silk dress. Luci screamed and struggled, but it was useless.

Mab and the fairies were invisible to these cruel men. They had no idea that there was an army of fairies, led by the Queen. It would prove to be their undoing. Queen Mab was furious at what was unfolding in front of her. Just as Luci was about to be thrown into the truck, Mab raised her arms, and summoned all the spirits of the sky, and the animals in the forest. Suddenly, black clouds appeared; day was turned into night, and the earth began to shake worse than a violent earthquake. The wind howled, the sky turned a sickly green, and within seconds the twisting clouds formed into a tornado. It kicked up dust and debris from the burned fields blinding the men who thrashed about trying to clear their eyes. The spirits began a high-pitched scream that was louder than the howling wind. The earsplitting shriek made the men's ears bleed. A pounding, stinging rain and hail pelted Luci's captors and quickly turned the ground into thick mud. As the men struggled with the screeching wind, the rain and mud, what happened next terrified them men even further.

From the jungle, there emerged animals of every kind: twenty jaguars, anaconda and pit viper snakes, hundreds of monkeys, large and small, bullet ants by the hundreds of thousands, thousands of poisonous Brazilian Wandering Spiders. These jungle creatures surrounded the men and the truck while the wind and rain beat mercilessly down on them. If this weren't enough, Mab called out the most fearsome curse of the fairy world upon the leader of the band of men, "*Sit autem omnis homo est lapis cor unum facti sunt!*" ("Let any man with a heart of stone become one.") Instantly, the leader was turned to stone. His eyes were bulging, and his mouth was wide open in a final scream. Even his fire stick had turned to stone. To this day, that statue remains an ominous reminder of the curse of the fairies.

The gang had seen enough. The legends were true! They had upset the spirits of the forest. All they could do now was to escape, but the mud had become as thick as quicksand. Try as they might, Luci's would-be kidnappers could not free themselves from the muck. As they struggled, the animals of the jungle descended on them. Several of them were bitten by the venomous snakes, by the jaguars, bullet ants and spiders. Their screams could be heard as they struggled to run in the knee-deep mud, but to no avail. All of them perished, but one. The man holding Luci dropped her into the mud, and ran, but not before he was captured by one of the anacondas that quickly coiled around the terrified man squeezing him within seconds of death. Although he could not see the Queen of the Fairies, the terrified man heard her voice above the din of the wind.

"I will let you live so that you can tell the others never to attempt to enter any further into our sacred jungle. That stone statue of your leader is the boundary. Go no further! Now go!" The large snake uncoiled, but before doing so, bit off the hand that had held Luci. The man screamed at the bite but managed to stumble away into the driving rain.

Queen Mab raised her arms again and called out to the spirits and the jungle animals, "Thank you, my friends. Our dear Luci is safe. The danger has passed. Peace." Immediately the clouds disappeared; the wind and rain stopped, and the animals retreated into the deep jungle.

Luci was sitting in a pile of mud. Her beautiful silk dress was in tatters. She was bruised, stunned and covered in mud. Her head was bleeding where she hit her head on the truck when the man dropped her. Queen Mab and the fairies immediately surrounded Luci.

From her haze, she managed to ask, "Mother, is Kisha alright?"

"Yes, child. He will have a headache for several days, but otherwise he is okay. Now, we need to take care of you."

Chapter 19

From Child to Young Woman

The following months and years passed peacefully. Luci's life was filled with laugher, love and joy. At sixteen, she was a brilliant runner, swimmer and tree climber. Her golden hair and flowing silk dress fluttered in waves as she ran along the paths. She could run almost as fast as the jaguars, certainly faster than Kisha, who was now growing old and could barely keep up with Luci's blinding pace. She teased him as he struggled to keep up, "Ha, you can't catch me, Kisha. That means you can't eat me."

However, Kisha had the last word. The aging jaguar responded in between heaving breaths, "My…dear… Luci, perhaps, not me…but the young jaguars. You…would…be a tasty morsel…"

Luci stopped in her tracks, and turned to Kisha, hands on her hips in a mock display of annoyance, "See, there you go again!"

The flower and fruit fairies had taught her about the richness of the jungle that provided all her needs for food and drink. Every day, the flower fairies put different flowers in Luci's hair, and enjoyed plaiting it. She played mathematics games with them, and although she lost every time, she did enjoy the challenge as much as her sisters. She was a voracious reader who loved history and had mastered several languages. The librarian in the nearby village had now grown accustomed to her books periodically disappearing, and then reappearing after several weeks or months, depending on the subject. In the place where the books had disappeared, there appeared a large basket of fruits and fragrant flowers. In fact, so accustomed had the librarian become to these mysterious events (and the fruit basket!), that she convinced the village council to order more books.

Perhaps, Luci's favourite time of day was in the evening. The heat and humidity in the forest had cooled. Luci, Queen Mab, and all the fairies would gather to talk and sing songs. The sweet sound carried through the jungle putting all the creatures at rest. She interrupted the music with a question she had long wanted to ask.

"Mother, you told me that my birth mother, Sira, disappeared in the jungle when she could not find me. Do you think, perhaps, one of these days, we can look for her? It makes me sad to think that she was so heartbroken that she lost her will to live."

The Fairy Queen saw the sadness in the young girl's eyes. She replied, "I understand, my child. You are now old enough to face the truth of what happened to her. We can certainly look for her. In the meantime, I shall ask the tree fairies to begin an investigation into your mother's disappearance. Then we can make a plan to find her. Do you understand that the outcome might be very unpleasant?"

"Yes, Mother, I understand. I am ready," Luci replied.

"Very well." Mab summoned several fairies, tree spirits and Bisha, the eagle. She asked each to begin the search for Sira, Luci's mother. She turned to Luci, and said, "The search will begin. Now we wait. Sleep now. Sweet dreams."

"Thank you, Mother. Good night."

Chapter 20

Maria Gloria

Maria Gloria Gilbert was the town librarian. Although old now, Mrs. Gilberto had been a former actress and a prominent member of the community. She went to university in Brasilia, the capital of Brazil to study science, and became an outstanding teacher. Later, she was an outspoken legislator whose mission was to preserve and protect the environment of her country. She had also become a wife and mother. However, her happiness was interrupted upon the deaths of both her husband of 25 years and her young son from malaria, a terrible disease found in the jungles of Brazil. Maria lived alone in an apartment near the library, Biblioteca Paulo

Sarmento, where she had been appointed chief librarian. The town of Humaita was at the edge of the State of Amazona in Brazil. The library was a small unassuming building that served both as a library and occasionally an air-conditioned meeting place for the villagers to escape the heat and humidity of the Amazon. For Gloria, every day was much the same: surrounded by books, and whispered voices. This was her sanctuary. The same few people came in day after day. Most people in this town were laborers in the nearby fields and had little free time to read. The children in the local school were the only frequent visitors.

Little did she know that today her life was about to change.

Maria Gloria made the walk to the library as she had for the past twenty years. When she went to put her key in the lock, she found that the door was already unlocked. Strange, she thought. I'm certain that I locked it before I left yesterday evening. She entered cautiously. Perhaps there were vandals in the building. No, can't be. Why would vandals be in a library? When she went to her office, she noticed that there was only one person, a young girl, sitting alone. The table was piled high with books, and the person was clearly immersed in a book. With a mix of concern and curiosity, she approached the girl. For a moment, the elderly librarian was stunned. She had never seen such a beautiful girl. Her hair was blonde and flowed like silk that hung over her shoulders down to her waist. Her skin was pale - as white as the petals on a daisy. She wore a silk yellow dress that shimmered in the morning light.

She had never seen anything, or for that matter, anyone like this. The librarian spoke to her in Portuguese, the language of Brazil. "Hello, young lady. How did you get in here, and what are you doing?"

The young girl decided not to reply to the question of how she got in. Her sister fairies had seen to that. As to the second question, Luci replied in perfect Portuguese, "I'm studying the Amazon forest, the people, the cultures, and the effect of logging, mining and agriculture on the future of the forest." The librarian was stunned by this girl's fluency in the language, and by her interest in the Amazon.

"I have never seen you here before? Where are you from?" the librarian asked with a raised eyebrow.

"From the rainforest," Luci replied simply.

The librarian wasn't satisfied. "Where in the forest?"

"I don't know, just the rainforest. It's my home with my sisters."

"You have sisters?"

Luci smiled and turned to the librarian. Her beautiful blue eyes and pale skin were captivating. "Yes, many, many sisters, and our animal friends."

It suddenly struck the librarian. She could hardly believe it. The mystery was solved! She immediately recalled the disappearance and re-appearance over the years of her books, and the fruit baskets. The open library door, the pile of books, the perfect language, a strange and beautiful girl from the forest with many sisters and friends. "You're one of the fairies, aren't you? You are the one who has been coming to borrow my books."

"I'm sorry, dear lady, if my sisters offended you. They were only trying to help me learn the ways of this world. No, I am not a fairy. My name is Luci." Her voice was soft and gentle, like the song of a morning bird.

At that instant, the frightened woman heard a voice. "Don't be afraid, Mrs. Gilberto. I am Mab, and this young lady is Luci, my daughter. She means you no harm, nor do my other children – the fairies. She only wishes to learn the ways of the world."

The stunned librarian was speechless. Her world began to spin around, at which point she fainted. Immediately, the fairies came to the poor woman's rescue. A cool, wet cloth appeared, and they applied it to her forehead. They buzzed around Mrs. Gilberto's head, singing sweet songs, and putting fragrant flowers under her nose. After a few minutes, the librarian stirred, mumbling a prayer. Luci helped her up. The librarian was now staring into the eyes of this mysterious, but beautiful vision. Her eyes were deep blue, her skin was pale, and her hair flowed like corn silk down to her waist. But it was the expression on the girl's face that captivated the librarian. She had a peaceful face with a gentle smile. The woman quickly felt the warmth all over her body. Luci helped her to her feet, and to a chair.

"Thank you, Luci, I feel much better."

"I will leave you now, dear lady. I am very sorry for the trouble I caused you."

Mrs. Gilberto replied smiling, "Luci, it is no trouble whatsoever. You will always be welcome here at any time."

During the following months, Luci and Mrs. Gilberto became good friends. She and Mrs. Gilberto enjoyed their discussions on a wide variety of subjects. Luci had a strong desire to learn. She could be seen in the early morning hours in the library surrounded by a mountain of books. The librarian introduced Luci to newspapers and helped her to understand current affairs. The young girl found it difficult to understand why people were so cruel and violent to one another; and why there were wars and conflicts.

"I don't understand, Mrs. Gilberto. Is it like this all the time?"

Mrs. Gilberto sighed deeply. She didn't want to infect the life of such an innocent and pure person with cynicism and distrust, but she did owe her the truth.

"I'm afraid so, child, but I have found that there are more good people than bad. Unfortunately, we only hear about the bad ones."

It saddened Luci, and only made her want to return to the safety and simplicity of her life in the jungle with her fairy sisters, and her mother, Queen Mab.

Chapter 21

The Changeling

It had been on her mind for several years, but she didn't feel that she could ask this unusual question. At first, she thought that Mab might be upset; or that the other fairies might think her too bold to ask such a thing. Luci was deep in thought to the point where the sounds of the jungle had faded from her hearing.

"My child is there something wrong. You look troubled," said the Queen.

"Well, I was thinking…."

"Yes?'

"Well, you know…"

The other fairies also noticed that Luci was troubled. They began to buzz in alarm. This was not at all like their beloved Luci.

"I'm listening. Go ahead. Speak your mind," Mab said with an uncharacteristic wrinkle in her brow.

"You won't be angry, will you, Mother?"

"First, how can I be angry if I don't know what you have done to make me angry. Second, and most important, I could never be angry with you," came Mab's reply.

Luci took a deep breath. "Here goes… You promise not to be angry with me?"

"I promise," came the Queen's response.

"Okay. Mother, I have learned so much from you, and my sisters," Luci started hesitatingly. She looked over to Mab and the other fairies. There was complete silence. They were waiting…

"Well, Mother, I have learned so much from you and my sisters…."

"You already said that," replied Queen Mab with a gentle smile. Ah, yes, the Queen thought. She now realised where this was going. *I am surprised that it took this long, Mab said to herself.* "Go on, Luci."

"Well, it's like …like …uh." She couldn't hold it in any longer. She blurted out, "I want to be a fairy."

The Queen smiled. The fairies buzzed in excitement and proceeded to express their agreement with unusual excitement. Out of nowhere, the fairies of the trees, the water, and the flowers showered Luci with leaves; sprinkled water; and poured thousands of beautiful coloured flowers over her.

Kisha, who was now old and unsteady on his feet, heard the commotion, and shuffled out of the bushes. "My dear Luci," said the old jaguar, "You wish to be a fairy? Then, I won't see you every day. You will be invisible like the others."

"I will always make myself visible to you, my dear Kisha."

"Thank you, but I was hoping that the young jaguars might have a chance to eat…."

"Don't you say it, Kisha." Luci frowned, and then said, "Why do you always think about eating…especially me?"

"Just kidding, just kidding," Kisha said with a smirk.

"Kisha…," Mab cautioned with a scowl. The old jaguar grumbled and sat with a groan to watch the proceedings.

The fairy queen continued. Her voice was solemn, "Luci, what you are asking is very serious. Once done, it cannot be reversed. Your life will be very different. Are you absolutely certain?"

"Yes, Mother, I have never been more certain about anything."

"Very well, then. We will begin the ceremony at first light."

Luci could hardly sleep with excitement: the thought that in several hours her life would change, change entirely and forever. Even her sister fairies were in a high state of anticipation at the prospect. It seemed that the entire jungle was awake, waiting for the ceremony to begin. Only Mab and Kisha were sound asleep.

At last, a few rays of light managed to break through the dense jungle canopy and settled on the moist floor. It was the signal of a new day – a very special day. It was the day that the changeling, Luci, would realise her long-held dream. Luci had been awake long before the light. She couldn't contain her excitement, nor could her sister fairies for that matter. They kept her company throughout the night by surrounding Luci in sparkles of light. They were unusually quiet, not wanting to wake the Queen Mother and Kisha, unlike their usual buzzing and giggling. Finally, Luci couldn't wait any longer. She rose from her sleeping mat, and ever so quietly walked to where Mab was sleeping. She stood there for the longest time, weighing her excitement against not wanting to disturb her mother. The decision was made for her: a mass of the fairies gathered around the queen and started buzzing. The queen awoke; Kisha was snoring.

"Good morning, Luci. I see your sisters are as excited as you are. Shall we awaken our furry friend here? His snoring even kept me awake." Mab leaned over and tickled Kisha's whiskers. The old jaguar opened one eye. "Really? Was that necessary? I was in the midst of a dream surrounded by delicious morsels all waiting to be eaten."

"It's time, Kisha. Our Luci is ready for the change. You have played a large part in how she got here. You don't want to sleep through this ceremony, do you? There will be time for eating later."

"Er, well, no, I guess. Okay, eat later." Kisha rose slowly, shook the cobwebs out of his head, and slowly stretched each leg. He was ready.

Mab beckoned for Luci to step closer to her. "Let us begin."

The Queen of the Fairies then closed her eyes; raised her arms; and began to sing an incantation, one that stretched back into the midst of time, a time when the spirits were the first to populate the earth. The fairies hummed in unison.

"I call upon the Goddess, Mother Earth to visit us. Our child, Luci, wishes her spirit to soar among the earth, moon, sun and stars, to become one with the rain, earth wind, and fire..."

Suddenly, the jungle was then transformed into a garden paradise, bathed in a golden light. Flowers sprang up, butterflies and birds of all kinds fluttered, and the rain forest creatures formed a large circle around Mab and Luci.

"...to take her place as sister to the spirits of the universe, the fairies and all the creatures of the Earth, and to protect the trees, the birds and all other life forms from harm. This, dear Mother Earth, is Luci's solemn request joined by all the spirits, fairies, and me..." The Queen continued her chant whilst gently rocking back and forth. Luci remained still, eyes closed and arms at her sides.

There was a sudden flash; a ball of light surrounded Luci. It began to swirl round and round, faster, faster until the young girl had disappeared in the whirling wind. Then there came bolts of lightning, first one, then another, and another, followed by a thunderous voice calling Luci's name. **"Luci, Luci, pure of heart and soul, friend and companion to the creatures of the earth, do you wish to join the spirits of the land, sister to the fairies? Is this your desire?"**

Then, the air became still; nothing moved. The cloud that surrounded Luci disappeared. A warm, golden light enfolded her in its place, revealing her draped in a glowing dress in a rainbow of colours. Her hair seemed to float in every direction giving the impression of a halo. Her pale white skin reflected the glow.

Time had been commanded to stand still to await her response. Luci's voice was soft, but firm as she raised her arms toward the sky above, "Yes, it is my desire."

A booming voice responded.

"So be it. Henceforth, you shall be called Princess of the Enchanted Forest."

A blinding flash of light and a rush of wind enveloped the entire area. When it passed, Luci had been completely transformed. She hovered in the air, surrounded by a halo of light that made her wings glisten. Her skin was so bright that it seemed translucent. Her hair was now a dazzling white beneath the ring of daisy flowers on her head. Her blue-green eyes sparkled like stars and her smile was warm and radiant, more than ever.

Queen Mab glided over to the new fairy and put her arms around her. She said gently, "Welcome, my child, to the world of fairies, enchantment and beauty. You and your sisters are the guardians of the forests, flowers, birds, butterflies, trees and streams, and all the creatures inhabiting it. This has been my wish for you for all these years. I am pleased."

Her sister fairies surrounded her. To her amazement, she now understood them! They were all chattering at the same time, offering their congratulations. Daisy Fairy spoke for all her sisters, "Dear sister, we are so happy for you. We always knew that this day would come. It is a joy to welcome you as our new sister." With that, Daisy Fairy gave a kiss on Luci's cheek, giggled and then flew off.

Kisha ambled over to the new fairy who was greeting the forest creatures before she would join her invisible sister fairies. He licked her hand as a sign acknowledging her new status. "Princess of the Rainforest, eh. My, you have come a long way, child. And to think, I wanted to eat you."

Luci kneeled down and put her cheek next to his, "Ha, don't ever change, my dear friend."

Finally, Kerwani, the alpha female monkey, walked over to Luci. "My dear Luci. I remember trying to carry you into the trees to protect you from that irritating cat over there, Kisha, until I couldn't carry you any longer. Now you don't need to climb the trees to visit me. You can fly!"

The celebrations continued long into the night. It was a cacophony of bird music from every bird in the jungle. The fairies danced with Luci while others played music. The wind added its own tune as it blew gently through the leaves and palm fronds. The monkeys sang their own song. Poor Kisha couldn't help himself. He joined the chorus with loud, hoarse, throaty roars that sounded more like gargling, and momentarily drowned out the beautiful music.

Queen Mab watched the merriment. She smiled, "Yes, my dear Luci, this has been my wish for you for all these years."

Chapter 22

The Search

Luci listened carefully to the reports from her sister fairies, the wind and the creatures in the jungle about the results of their search for Luci's mother, Sira. With each disappointing report, Queen Mab urged everyone to widen their search. "We must know her fate, my sisters, my friends. Our dear Luci has waited so long."

And so, the search continued week after a long week. As time went on with the same empty report, Luci could not help being discouraged, but she never gave up hope of finding her mother. She could accept her mother's fate, but, at least, she could put an end to the question

that had plagued her for so long. It would be closure –
one way or the other.

It was the rainy season. The jungle came alive with
each downpour. The fragrances that arose from the
forest floor were intoxicating. The sweet aroma of
millions of blooming flowers, shrubs of every variety
mingled with the smell of dense, wet vegetation and
decaying wood. Torrents of water cascaded through
what once were little streams, turning them into raging
rivers. The jungle was reborn after each rainfall when the
sun came from behind the thundering clouds. The lush
green returned; the steam rose high into the trees and
beyond. The rains brought danger, but exquisite beauty.

After one of these cloudbursts, a group of excited
fairies flew to Mab who was seated on her flower throne
speaking with Luci. The fairies were speaking
simultaneously, and so fast that it startled the Queen.

"My children, slow down; one at a time. I see you
have some exciting news. Daisy Fairy, please, go on."

Daisy Fairy could hardly contain herself. Her sister fairies were encouraging her to "get on with it." She didn't know where to start.

"Well, dear Mother, we were flying near…"

Rose Fairy interrupted, "Never mind that, tell her what we found, dear sister."

"Well, dear Mother, we saw…"

Lily Fairy could no longer wait for the whole story to be spun, "Dear Mother, I think we found Luci's mother."

Daisy Fairy, the most intellectual of the fairies, said, "With respect, dear sister, we found evidence of someone in or near the cave where Luci was once abandoned."

Luci jumped up. She could hardly contain herself. "Please dear sisters. Tell me everything. Every detail. Is it possible that she's alive?"

Queen Mab gently put her hand on Luci's shoulder. "We must remain calm, my child. Let your sisters finish their report. We will go from there."

The fairies began their report: during the dry season, the brook that ran alongside the cave where Luci was abandoned was shallow. Once the rainy season came, however, that brook became a furious and mighty river that flooded over the cave. Whatever or whoever was in that cave could not have survived the flood. Or at least that's what everybody thought. After the rain stopped, the flood receded, and the river once again returned to a peaceful, gentle burbling brook - until the next downpour. During that brief pause when the rain clouds gave way to the sun, the fairies saw the cave, and what appeared to be ragged clothes at the outside of the cave.

Daisy Fairy finished the report, "It would be impossible for those clothes, or what appeared to be clothes, to have been deposited there by a raging river of water. That is why we concluded that someone must have survived, and is in the cave, or at least near it, and using it for shelter. We did not go in the cave but came directly here."

Luci was so excited that she could hardly breathe. "Mother, can we go now? This could be the moment that I've waited for."

"Yes, my child. We can go now, but remember, we must accept what we find," Mab cautioned.

As the group of fairies was about to leave, Kisha ambled over. He was very old now, and walking took all his energy. "My dear Luci, I hope you find your mother."

Luci knelt down and stroked the old jaguar behind his ears. He liked that. "Thank you, Kisha. I hope we find her. It has been so long." Kisha said, "I am old now, and cannot make the journey. So, I have asked the young jaguars to accompany you to protect you."

Then to Luci's surprise, Kisha added, "I had a mother once. I'm afraid I was a disappointment to her."

Luci responded, "That's impossible. You are… well, you are you."

Kisha continued, "My mother always said that I put my stomach before my paws."

She had to suppress a laugh. She replied, "Well, my friend, you do have an obsession about food."

"I was supposed to be walking with her," Kisha said wistfully, "but I couldn't help myself. There was this beautiful deer just waiting to be eaten. I stalked the deer from behind, and then pounced. Well, just as I was about to get my claws into her backside, that deer bucked, and kicked me in the teeth. I lost a tooth and broke my jaw. I couldn't growl, grumble, eat or drink for weeks. Rather than starve to death, my mother made me eat earthworms. Ugh, disgusting!" Kisha shook his head as if trying to clear his head of a bad memory.

Luci couldn't stand it any longer. She burst out laughing. "Earthworms. Your mother made you eat earthworms? How awful for you."

"And my breath was so bad that no one would come near me."

Luci patted the forlorn jaguar's head. "Well, that explains a lot, my friend. Thank you for sharing." With that, the search party departed, leaving poor Kisha by the stream drinking water as if to wash his mouth from the memory of earthworms.

Fairies could travel enormous distances in a blink of an eye. The remainder of the group traveled overland for several hours. They arrived at the cave but there were no clothes to be seen. The fairies settled in front of the opening. The Queen decided to wait until the jaguars arrived before entering the cave. As the fairies had now assumed a physical presence, they could be injured or worse.

The jaguars – five of them – arrived after having run many miles. They emerged from the jungle thickness as silently as they entered it. "My Queen, we are ready," said the leader of the group bowing his head. His name was Tambo. He was the largest of any of the jaguars in the jungle, and the successor to Kisha. Tambo was both intelligent and fearless.

"Thank you, Tambo," said the Queen. "Please be careful."

Tambo signaled to his companions. Slowly and stealthily, they entered the cave. Within a few steps, they disappeared into the darkness. The cats kept low to the ground and measured every step. With their incredibly sharp night vision, they were able to navigate their way even in the pitch dark. It was evident to the jaguar team that the cave was larger and more complex than might have appeared at the simple entrance. They went from one chamber to the next, scanning from left to right, looking for any signs of life. Nothing. They pushed further and further into the blackness. They also noticed that the ground was rising. Tambo concluded that it was possible for someone to retreat into the recesses of this cave and be above the floodwaters during the heavy rains. Still, there were no signs of life.

The team of jaguars explored deeper and deeper inside the cave. How could it be possible for a human with limited night vision to manage to get this deep into the cave, given the distance and the darkness? Tambo was about to order a return when he noticed an unusual object. It was a small faded blue blanket, worn and ragged at the edges. They went further, continuing on the rising path until they saw a single shaft of light, and a rope ladder leading to the top of the cave. *So, that's how the person was able to avoid being discovered, and escape the rising waters of the stream,* Tambo thought. "We must return to report what we have found to the Queen," the big cat said.

Tambo and the other four jaguars began their retreat when they observed footprints leading off to one of the many passages. The five cats decided to follow the trail. It had become clear to them that a human with their limited sense of vision, hearing and smell could easily become lost in these bewildering, dark corridors. As they crept silently along this passageway, they suddenly stopped. It was a smell – one that they recognised. It was the same smell that Luci had. There was a human in this cave, and it was alive!

They pressed forward, more carefully now. Humans were terrified of jaguars, and this human could possess weapons similar to the ones they had encountered in the jungle clearing when they helped Luci escape from the evil men who wanted to take her. Slowly, stealthily, the cats moved. They didn't make a sound – even their breathing was silent.

The corridor opened into a large cavern. The cats lined up, side by side. If they had to attack, they would charge as one. However, what they saw shocked even these seasoned hunters. A dim glow was all that remained of a small campfire. Sitting with knees up and holding her legs was a slight, frail old woman. She sat huddled by the embers. When the jaguars moved forward, she saw them, and quickly backed up against the wall, putting her hands up in front of her in a vain gesture of self-defense.

The jaguars could see an old woman who wore dirty, tattered rags for clothes. Her white hair, knotted and tangled, hung down to her waist. Her face was wrinkled and drawn. Her skin was ghostly pale. She was thin to the point of being fragile. Clearly, this poor woman was starving and posed no threat.

Tambo said to his four companions, "Stay here, and watch her. I think this might be the human Luci has been searching. I will go back and report this to the Queen and to Luci."

The old woman could hear the jaguars' guttural rumble. Then to her surprise, she saw four of them lie down in front of her, and one, the largest, turn and disappear into the darkness. She could not know, but she could sense that these hunters were not going to attack – at least not yet. She sat motionless. The jaguars never took their menacing yellow eyes off her.

Chapter 23

The Reunion

"Mother, they have been in there for such a long time," Luci said. She was both concerned for the cats, and impatient to get some news.

"Be patient, Luci. They are the best hunters in the forest. They will explore the cave, and report back," the Queen replied calmly.

As if on cue, Tambo emerged from the cave. He squinted in the sunlight, and then turned to the Queen and to Luci. Luci ran over to him, and nearly fell on top of him. This was Tambo's first interaction with a "human", and he was unaccustomed to such close contact. He backed up and growled.

"I'm sorry," Luci said to the jaguar. "I'm just so anxious to learn what you found."

Tambo was satisfied with the apology but made a mental note to speak to Kisha about how he was able to put up with these emotional creatures.

Tambo reported what he and the team had found. He described the old woman, her tattered clothes, her condition, and the rope ladder in the upper chamber. "I will lead you back, but I suggest you bring her some food. She is in a bad state."

The Queen quickly organised for the fairies to collect water, fruits, nuts and berries. She ordered the fairies to enter the cave first and provide light for the group. They came together to form a large ball of light, making the cave as bright as day. With Tambo in the lead and the benefit of light, the group quickly progressed into the cave's depth.

When they reached the cavern, Tambo gave a low growl to alert the other four cats who were still crouched in front of the terrified old woman. Perhaps it was instinct or some other deep-rooted feeling, but Luci knew that they had found her mother. She rushed past the four cats and dropped to her knees in front of the old woman.

"Mother? It's me, Luci. I found you at last!"

The old woman who had not uttered a word in all these years could only make grunting noises. She had been alone for so long without seeing another human being that she became confused and frightened at the sight of this young woman, the fairies and the Queen. Hunger, solitude and despair had been her companions for such a long time that she could no longer imagine any other state. The old woman remained silent and vigilant, her eyes darting from one person to the other.

Luci waited for some sign of recognition, but there was nothing. The Queen came over and put a hand on Luci's shoulder, "She needs time, my child. We can only imagine the suffering she has endured. And assuming, of course, that this is your mother."

Luci replied, "Mother, I know she is my mother. I just know it!"

"Very well, let us feed this poor woman." The fairies laid the water, fruits and nuts in front of the woman, who hungrily attacked the food, stuffing as much as she could in her mouth. Luci, Mab, the fairies now visible to the poor woman and the jaguars watched in astonishment as the old woman ate the food and packed the remainder in her dirty dress. Throughout, she kept a wary eye on the intruders in her hideout.

As the woman sat eating, Tambo left the group, disappearing into the darkness. After a while, he reappeared with a faded blue blanket in his mouth. He laid it in front of the woman, who immediately snatched it away, and clutched it to her chest. She started to grunt and scream at the group, wildly waving her arms to keep them away.

Luci looked on in amazement. She had never seen anything like this. She felt sadness for this poor woman, but something told her that this was indeed her mother, and she needed to reach her. She turned to the fairy queen, "Mother, is there anything that we can do for her?"

Queen Mab gestured to the fairies who surrounded the poor woman in a warm glow. She then bent over the woman, gently touched her forehead, and in a whisper said, "Be calm, dear lady. All will be well." Instantly, the woman's shoulders drooped, and her head bent over. Her eyes closed as if she were asleep.

Luci bent closer to the old woman. "Do you remember your little girl – the one who was taken to this cave, and left to die? Do you remember my name? Luci, it's Luci. It's me."

The old woman opened her eyes, and looked intensely at Luci as if she were trying desperately to capture a long-lost memory. She struggled to make words. "L.. L…Luc….Luc…Luc, Luc." It was more a guttural, croaking sound than a name. She repeated the sound again and again. Finally, after long moments of struggling, the word was formed. "Luci… Luci, Luci." And then, as if a dark veil began to lift, some recognition began to return, slowly and painfully. The poor woman grimaced. She closed her eyes, and began to shake her head, trying desperately to remember. And then, she cried out in joy, "Luci? Luci? Is it really you?" Tears welled in her eyes.

"Yes. It's me. I'm Luci," came Luci's tearful reply. "I'm your daughter." Luci put her arms around the old woman. She could feel the bones in her mother's fragile body. She cradled her mother for several long moments. Both mother and daughter cried with a combination of joy for the discovery, and sorrow for the loss of so many years.

And then, the old woman took the worn blue blanket, and gently draped it over Luci's shoulders. In a raspy voice, she said, "My baby, my beautiful baby, Luci."

The woman looked around her. Now, more aware of her surroundings, she was confused. She raised a weak arm, and pointed to the fairies, Queen Mab and the jaguars. "Don't be afraid, mother. These are my sisters, my Queen Mother, and my friends. They rescued me from this cave, and I have been living with them since then. They are now my sisters. I am one of them."

The old woman slowly and painfully motioned to Mab and the fairies to come closer. In a halting voice, hardly above a hoarse whisper, she said, "Thank you… for…rescuing my baby,…Luci." She was exhausted physically and emotionally, but now finally happy. After so many long years of loneliness, heartache and despair, her search was over. She had found her daughter, her beloved Luci. She never believed that her daughter had perished in this cave. Her hopes and dreams were answered. Sira then put her head on Luci's shoulder and fell into a peaceful sleep.

When Sira awoke, she was startled by her new surroundings. She was no longer in the dismal cave, her home for so many years, but in a dense jungle surrounded by fairies, elegant trees, the most beautiful, fragrant flowers, and, of course, the ever-present jaguar, Kisha.

Luci and her sister fairies had prepared a feast for Sira to celebrate her return. They had helped her wash off the grime of the cave under a nearby waterfall and rubbed flower oil on her skin. Gone was the pallid grey, now replaced with a lustrous sheen. Another group of fairies cut her hair, then braided it as she requested. They topped off their handiwork with a crown of daisies. Finally, a larger group had finished a dress for their new "Luci mother." It was a pale blue, like the afternoon sky, with a blue belt that had been made from the remnants of the blue blanket that kept Sira company for all those years, and that had wrapped her baby Luci so long ago.

EPILOGUE

It was a quiet evening in the forest thicket – the home to the fairies of this enchanted place. The quiet was only broken by the buzzing of the fairies, the sounds of the chirping crickets, and the whispers of Queen Mab and Sira as they shared their memories of Luci. The Fairy Queen spoke of Luci's childhood, her education and adventures, her visits with Mrs. Gilberto at the library, and her adoption as a fairy. Sira listened with wide eyes; she could hardly believe it. There was still so much to take in. Her baby's life started out as a certain tragedy; but now, now she was the Fairy Princess of this enchanted forest. Luci slept on a pillow of ferns alongside her sister fairies, and the old greying jaguar,

Kisha who was the only animal permitted to see the fairies, Luci and Queen Mab.

As both mothers were speaking, the old jaguar got up and strolled over to Sira and Mab. The Queen introduced the big cat to Sira. "Lady Sira, this is Kisha, the self-appointed guardian of Luci." Still frightened of jaguars, Sira leaned back slightly, still unsure, until Kisha licked the old woman's hand in a sign of respect. The Queen Mother stroked the jaguar's head that was now white with age. "Kisha has been keeping watch over Luci since she was a baby. He wants you to know that he will stand by her for the rest of his life, and after he dies, another jaguar will take his place as Luci's guardian."

Sira was still amazed at all that was happening: her daughter, now a fairy, Luci's other mother, Queen Mab, the serene jungle with all the hundreds of other fairies, and the ever present guardian jaguar. Aware that people of the jungle had a primal fear of these large cats, Sira especially marveled at the rapport and loving relationship between Luci and Kisha. To Sira's surprise, Kisha then walked over to Luci and snuggled up against her. Luci stirred. She opened one eye and threw her arm around Kisha.

Night in the jungle settles like a dark blanket; the darkness was impenetrable, but for the music of the night. As Sira listened, she remembered the happy days in the village with her husband, Tulo. She still felt a sadness for him and the awful decision he had to make, which must have weighed so heavily on him. In the indistinct light, she could hear Luci's rhythmic breathing and the snoring of the old jaguar. She crawled slowly to her side and cuddled her the way she did as a baby. The ever-vigilant Kisha saw Luci's mother and for an instant tensed, but he remembered his own mother and those moments of warmth and security. He soon fell fast asleep.

Of course, Queen Mab could see the three figures in their embrace. "*Yes,*" she thought, *the circle is now closed. All will be well, all will be well.*"

About The Author

Philip Antony has drawn on his experiences from his multi-faceted career as a lawyer, business consultant and university professor. He has travelled the world where he was privileged to meet and interact with people of many cultures, which he has woven into all of his stories. He has produced a long line of young adult stories and adult novels in which his rich imagination and international experiences have created a cast of colourful, relatable characters and exciting adventures.

The underlying theme of his stories is the power of love, friendship and compassion that overcome the forces of hatred and division. Although his stories are works of fiction, his novels convey that contemporary message with excitement interspersed with warmth and humour. His work stands in stark contrast to the enmity and divisiveness we read about in our world today.